Beauty
and the
BEAST

Retold by
Michael Morpurgo

Illustrated by
Loretta Schauer

HarperCollins *Children's Books*

Beauty
and the
BEAST

For Kitty – M.M.
For Pam and Dave with love – L.S.

First published in paperback in Great Britain
by HarperCollins Children's Books in 2012
This edition published in 2013

3 5 7 9 10 8 6 4

ISBN: 978-0-00-751340-6

HarperCollins Children's Books is a division of
HarperCollins Publishers Ltd.

Text copyright © Michael Morpurgo 2012
Illustrations copyright © Loretta Schauer 2012

Visit our website at: www.harpercollins.co.uk

Printed and bound in China

For Marco and his wife and three daughters, life was sweet. They lived in a grand house in the city with all the comforts they could possibly wish for. They were healthy, wealthy and happy. He was a respected merchant of fine silks and tapestries and spices from the East. The future looked golden for all of them.

But then one spring Marco's wife died suddenly. So now Marco had to bring up his daughters all on his own. He did his very best to keep his daughters happy. He gave them everything they asked for, presents every time he came home. The two older sisters soon became very spoilt.

Only the youngest, Belle, remained loving and kind-hearted. She always hated it when her father went away on business. Whenever he wasn't there her sisters were always horrible to her. She cried herself to sleep every night, and longed every day for her father to come home.

So Belle was overjoyed to look out of her window one morning and see him come riding home sooner than she had expected. "Presents!" cried her sisters, and they all ran downstairs to greet him. But there were no presents.

Marco slumped down in his chair and told them the dreadful news. "All is lost," he said. "The ship from Istanbul, carrying all my silks and tapestries and spices, has been taken by pirates. We have no money. I shall have to sell all we have, this house, all our silver, everything, to pay my debts."

"But where will we live, Father?" Belle asked.

"I shall find somewhere, Belle," Marco told her. "But there will be no servants, no creature comforts. Those days are over."

"No servants!" the two older sisters protested. "How can we live without servants?"

"From now on," said their father, "we shall have to do everything for ourselves. We shall have to find a cottage high up in the mountains, and keep sheep and pigs. We shall have to grow all our own food."

"Mountains, sheep, pigs, how wonderful!" Belle cried. "We'll be fine, Father, we'll be fine." And her two sisters looked at her darkly, and hated her all the more.

For many years the family lived like peasants, struggling to survive high in their mountain cottage, Marco hunting and gathering wood, the three sisters working all day and every day looking after the sheep and pigs. There wasn't a day when her two older sisters did not groan and moan and gripe. Belle never complained, but it was a hard life.

"Things will get better one day, Belle," Marco kept telling her. But he didn't believe it, not really, and nor did she. Then one day things did get better.

Word came that the pirates who had stolen all Marco's silks and tapestries and spices had been captured, and all his goods recovered. He was overjoyed, the whole family was. As Marco prepared to leave for the coast to retrieve his lost possessions, he told his daughters, "By the time I come home, we shall be rich again. I can bring you whatever you like."

"Diamonds and emeralds and sapphires, lots and lots of them," said the two elder sisters.

"And you, Belle?" Marco asked. "What would you like me to bring for you?"

"A red red rose," Belle replied. "No roses grow up here. I love roses."

"All will be well again, my daughters," said Marco, and he rode away down to the coast.

But all was not well. When Marco arrived at the port he discovered that all the silks and tapestries and spices had been spoilt by sea-water. Everything was ruined and quite worthless. In deep despair he made his way back to the mountains, and on his way found himself lost in a great dark forest. Hungry and thirsty and cold, he lay down to sleep, wishing never to wake up again.

When he woke he looked up and saw through the trees the towers of a huge palace. As he came closer, he saw the front door was wide open, almost inviting him in, it seemed.

He found a huge log fire burning in the hearth, and a dining table laden with food and drink. He thought he must be in heaven itself. There were roasted meats and salted fish, succulent plums and plump pears, mountainous cakes and mouth-watering jellies. Marco sat down and helped himself, until he was full to bursting. Then he sat down in front of the fire and was soon fast asleep.

He woke to discover that the table had been laid for breakfast. This is just too good to be true, he thought, and helped himself again. Feeling much stronger now to face the journey, he left the palace and set off for home.

As he went on his way, he found himself in a beautiful rose garden, with red red roses growing all around. He remembered then what Belle had asked him to bring home. So he picked three roses, one for each of his daughters – that way he would have something for each of them.

The moment he picked the last rose, there appeared on the path, blocking his way, a hideous beast. Huge and horrible he was, cruel claws and foul breath, and narrow eyes that glared down at him. Marco was rooted to the spot with terror.

"First you steal my food," snarled the Beast – he had the voice of a wolf. "And now you steal my roses. For this you shall die!"

Marco fell to his knees and begged for mercy. "The food I took because I was starving," he cried. "And the roses I plucked for my daughters who have no one to care for them but me. Spare me for their sake, I beg you."

"You have daughters?" said the Beast.

"Three," replied Marco.

"Very well," the Beast went on, after some thought. "I will spare you, but only if you send me one of your daughters in your place. And you must not make her come. She must come of her own free will. If none of them will come, then you must promise to return yourself to face whatever fate I have in store for you. Do you promise?"

Marco promised. He had no choice, he knew that, not if he wanted to live. But all the way home he regretted his promise.

Belle was delighted to see him and loved her red red rose, but her sisters hated theirs. They threw them on the ground and stamped on them, screaming at Marco and cursing him for returning home as poor as he had left.

Belle found him later sitting amongst the sheep on the mountainside, head in his hands.

"They don't mean what they say, Father," she said, trying to comfort him.

"They do," Marco replied. "But it is not their words that are troubling me." And then he told her everything that had happened to him, and everything he had promised the Beast.

"I'll go, Father," she said at once. "I'll be kind to him, and he'll be kind to me because you kept your promise. Everyone is kind deep down. He won't hurt me. Why should he?"

Try as he did to persuade her not to go, Belle insisted. Her sisters of course, were only too pleased to be rid of her.

As it turned out, Belle was right. When she reached the palace that same evening, the Beast could not have been more welcoming and kind. She did not seem to mind one bit what he looked like, and the Beast loved her at once for that, and for her beauty too.

"My palace is your palace," he told her. "And I will be your willing servant. Ask whatever you like and it will be done. All I ask is that each night you allow me to ask you one question, the same question. You may answer how you like."

Every night, after long and happy days of talking and walking in the rose garden, the Beast would ask her the same question, "Dearest Belle, will you marry me?"

And every night she gave him the same answer, "Maybe, but can I think about it just a little longer?"

She did think about it too. She even dreamed about it, and in her dreams there was always a handsome prince who lived in a great palace, and who kept asking her that very same question, and she kept saying, maybe. The dreams seemed so real to her that when Belle woke up she was sure the prince must be somewhere close by, somewhere in the palace. That was why she started to imagine that perhaps the Beast might be keeping the prince locked up in one of the towers. She hoped and believed he could never do such a thing, but all the same she searched every room in the palace for the prince of her dreams, just to be sure. But the prince was not there.

In time the Beast became such a dear and trusted friend to her, that she told him all about her dreams and confessed to him how she'd searched the palace high and low. The Beast shook his head sadly. "There is no handsome prince here, only me," he told her, looking away so she could not see the tears in his eyes.

That night when the Beast asked her yet again to marry him, Belle had a different answer for him. "Dear friend, you have been so kind and patient. I promise faithfully that in one week I shall let you know. But before I make up my mind once and for all, I should like to ask my father. He is the wisest man I know. Would you mind if I went home for a few days to see him, to see my family? I love being here with you, but I do miss them."

The Beast did not want her to go, but neither did he want to keep her against her will – he loved her too much for that. "Go then," he told her, "but keep your promise and be back in a week with your answer or you will break my heart. And take these with you." He gave Belle an enchanted mirror and a magic ring. "Look into this mirror and you will always be able to see me and talk to me whenever you like. As for this ring, you only have to turn it three times around your finger and in the same breath you will be back here with me."

The next morning Belle left for the mountains. The Beast watched her go with heavy heart, longing already to see her again the moment she was out of sight. Back at home in the cottage, Belle sat by the fire and told her father all about her wonderful life in the Beast's palace: how the Beast loved her and wanted to marry her and make her his princess, and how she had promised faithfully she would be back inside a week to give him her answer, and she showed him the enchanted mirror and the magic ring the Beast had given her. Marco told her she should go where her heart led her, back to the palace to be with the Beast who loved her so much.

All this her two sisters overheard. They were seething with jealousy. Who did Belle think she was, coming home and showing off in all her silken finery? Why should she have all the comforts of life while they had to stay home looking after the sheep and pigs? They would see to it that their little sister never returned to her palace, never became a princess. So they stole her mirror and her ring and hid them high in a crow's nest in the old oak tree by the stream. Belle looked everywhere for them, but could not find them.

Then, knowing the kindness of Belle's heart, they thought up a cunning way of making her stay at home, and so break her promise. Every morning as Belle was about to leave, they rubbed onion skins in their eyes so that they could not stop themselves from crying. "Do not go, sister dear," they cried, the tears rolling down their cheeks. "Stay, please stay!" And every time the trick worked, just as they had hoped and planned. A week and a day went by, then another day and another, and still Belle could not bring herself to leave her weeping sisters.

Every night Belle dreamed again about her handsome prince, only now the dream ended differently. Now she was telling him, "Yes dearest, I will marry you!" But then one night she had a different dream altogether. She saw her sisters climbing the old oak tree by the stream. They were hiding away her mirror and her ring high up in a crow's nest.

She woke, ran down to the stream, climbed the tree, and found the mirror and the ring in the nest. There and then she looked into the mirror, and she saw her beloved Beast lying in the rose garden of the palace, a red red rose in his hand. He lay there as still as death. With three twists of the ring on her finger she was kneeling at his side, crying her heart out. As her tears fell on his face, as she kissed his leathery lips, the Beast was suddenly a beast no more, but the handsome prince of her dreams. And when his eyes opened and he smiled up at her, she was filled with such happiness that she thought her heart would burst.

They sat in the rose garden together, and told one another all the whys and wherefores they needed to know, how Belle's horrible sisters had tricked her into not keeping her promise, how the prince had been stolen away by an evil fairy when he was a little boy because she wanted a child of her own, how he had tried to run away from her and been turned into a hideous beast, a curse that could only be lifted if he was ever touched by tears of true love. And now he had been!

Belle and her handsome prince married soon after, and in the rose garden too. What a wedding it was! Everyone came from miles around. They sang and danced and feasted through the night, till the stars faded, till the moon became the sun. Her father was there of course, and the sisters too – Belle had long since forgiven them for the wrong they had done her. The whole family came to live in the palace – there was plenty of room after all. And as it turned out, the sisters proved to be wonderful aunties to Belle's seven children.

But just to remind them of how horrible they had once been, if ever they needed onions to be cut up for soups and stews, Belle always made her sisters do it. And they wept buckets every time!